NICK BUTTERWORTH AND MICK INKPEN

THE FOX'S TALE

Sometimes, grown-ups find it hard to believe in miracles. In Nick Butterworth and Mick Inkpen's delightful *Animal Tales*, special occasions in Jesus' life are seen through the eyes of some of God's smaller creatures, who have no trouble at all understanding exactly what is happening...

Marshall Pickering is an Imprint of
HarperCollins*Religious*
Part of HarperCollins*Publishers*
77-85 Fulham Palace Road, London W6 8JB

First published in Great Britain
in 1988 by Marshall Pickering

This edition published in 1994

Text and illustrations Copyright © 1988
Nick Butterworth and Mick Inkpen

The authors and illustrators each assert the moral right to be
identified as the authors and illustrators of this work

A catalogue record for this book is
available from the British Library

ISBN 0 551 02877-7

Printed and bound in Hong Kong

NICK BUTTERWORTH AND MICK INKPEN

THE FOX'S TALE

JESUS IS BORN

Hello, I'm a fox. I live out on the hills.
I sleep by day and hunt by night.

If you're lucky you might see me on
a hilltop against the moon. But don't
blink or I'll be gone.

Here's my story. It'll make your tail
bristle. Listen.

Two nights ago I'm up on the hill near the town. The night is cold and clear. I lift my head and sniff the air. The scent of sheep is everywhere.

There's another smell too. It halts me in my tracks. The shepherd's out ... by my nose more than one. That means the sheep are lambing.

I skirt around the hill, then wait a while, and listen. Somewhere up ahead a lamb is calling to its mother.

Crouching low and keeping to the bushes I follow. Now I can see it clearly sitting in the long grass. A speckled lamb, not one week old.

Suddenly a blinding flash sends me running to the bushes. Shaking to my toes and blinking in the light, I freeze.

Across the hill a golden glow has fallen. And coming from the sky the sound of singing.

All at once the air is filled with shining men!

I'm scared. I cannot smell these men. They have no scent.

One of them is speaking to the shepherds.

'Don't be afraid,' he says. 'We bring good news. Great joy has come to all of you. Today in Bethlehem a baby has been born. He is your promised King, your Saviour. You'll find him lying in a cattle trough. Quickly, run and see!'

Suddenly, the shining men are gone.
The sound of singing dies away.

The shepherds stare at one another.
Then all at once they start to talk.

They laugh and shout. They jump
and clap their hands. Then off they run
towards the town to find the baby King.
I follow on behind.

I am wary of the town. It's full of sounds and smells I do not know. But I would like to see this baby King.

Keeping to the shadows I watch the shepherds disappear inside a stable.

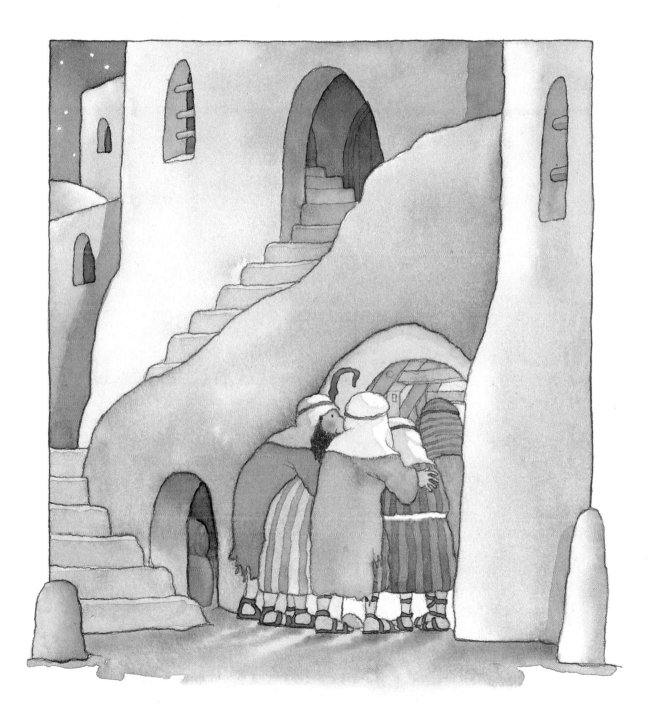

Behind the stable is a high fence.
Without a sound I'm up and over it.

My luck is in. There is light
streaming through a crack in the back
wall. From here I can see everything.

Inside are cows and sheep and goats. It's odd. They know I'm here but they are not afraid.

There are people too. A woman and a man, and by the door the shepherds. All of them are looking at a cattle trough lit by a lantern.

And there, just as the shining men said, a new-born baby sleeps. A King in a cattle shed.

His mother smiles and tells the shepherds to come in. Quietly they stand and watch. The baby murmurs in his sleep.

'His name is Jesus,' says the woman softly.

One of the shepherds takes something from his cloak. It is the speckled lamb. A present for the baby.

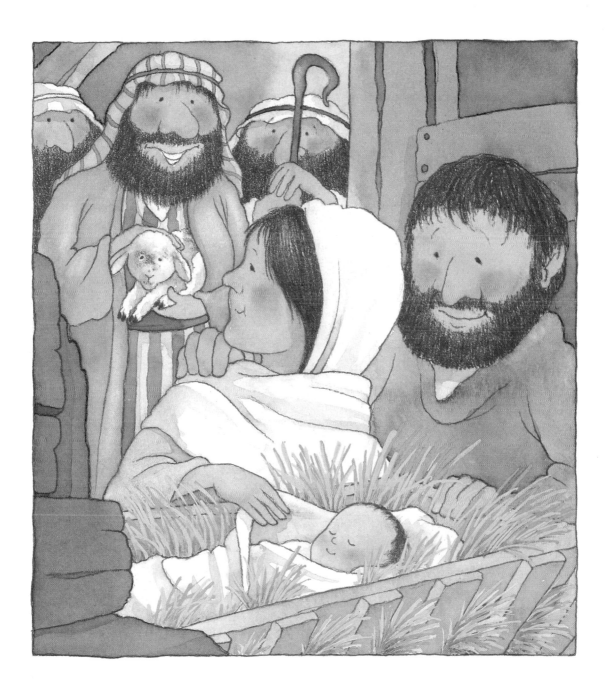

He gives it to the woman, then bends close to see the baby's face.

The shepherd's smiling face glows in the light, just like the shining men. He has seen a King and so have I. Not many shepherds or foxes can say that.

The shepherds whisper their goodbyes and leave.

My belly tells me that I too must be making tracks. It is a harsh winter and life is hard for a fox. And for you too, little King, it seems.

I wish you well. I hope the lamb will keep you warm. Sweet dreams.

If you enjoyed this *Animal Tale*,
you can also read

The Cat's Tale – Jesus at the Wedding

The Magpie's Tale – Jesus and Zacchaeus

The Mouse's Tale – Jesus and the Storm